This Little Tiger book belongs to:

_____

_____

_____

Don't be so nosy, Posy!

Nicola Grant   Tim Warnes

LiTTLE TiGER
LONDON

Posy the piglet didn't mean to be nosy. She was just terribly interested in knowing things.

"Who wakes *you* up each morning?" she asked Ronny Rooster.

"Does it hurt to lay an egg?" she said to Hetty Hen.

"Questions, questions!" the animals sighed. "Don't be so nosy, Posy!"

But Posy wanted to learn things. Even if it did sometimes land her in trouble!

One morning, Posy was playing "don't tread on the daisies" with Cowslip Cow. As they skipped under an oak tree, they heard a strange noise.

"I wonder what that is?" said Posy, peering inside a hollow in the oak to look.

"Oooh! Don't do that, Posy!" cried Cowslip, but it was too late . . .

ZZZZZZZZZZZZZZZZZZZ!

Posy raced off quickly, chased
by some very cross bees!
"Oh Posy, you do look funny!"
Cowslip laughed. "You've got
honey all over your nosy nose!"

The next day, Posy was playing in the farmyard when she spotted the farmer's tractor nearby.

"I wonder what *this* does?" she said, pressing a big red button.

BEEEEEEP! blasted the horn. Posy tumbled out in a heap!

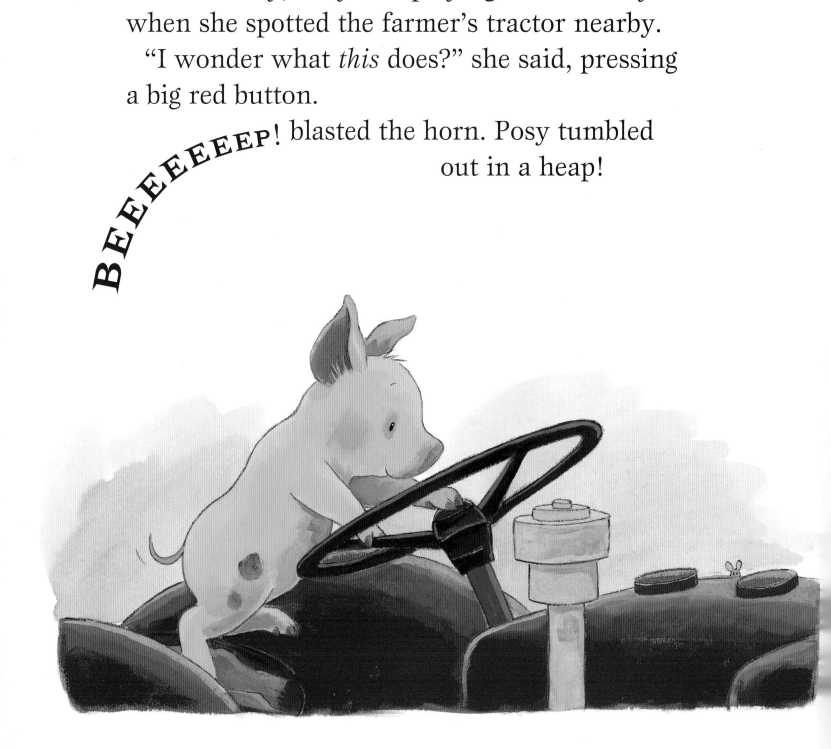

"Who's playing with my tractor?" yelled the farmer, running up.

"It's Nosy Posy!" clucked Hetty Hen crossly. "And she's woken me from my nap!"

"Sorry!" Posy squealed. "I'll try to play more quietly!"
But Posy couldn't stay quiet for long!

"Do you feel chilly without your warm woolly fleece?" she asked Sally Sheep on shearing day.

"Tell me, do you keep noses in your nose-bag?" she laughed at Harry Horse.

"How silly!" mumbled Harry. "One day you'll learn not to be so nosy, Posy!"

But Posy didn't think so!

Then, one sunny day, Posy and Dilly and Dally Duck were playing piggybacks. "Ooooooooooh!" came a strange noise from somewhere across the field. "Sshh!" whispered Posy. "What was that?"

"Ooooooooooooooooooooooooooooooooh!" came the ghostly cry again, even louder!

"Let's find out what it is!" Posy said excitedly.

"Don't be nosy, Posy!" quacked Dilly and Dally. "Whatever it is, it sounds scary!"

"Scaredy ducks!" Posy laughed back. "Come on!"

Posy ran across the field, with Dilly and Dally tiptoeing behind.

A large, dark shape loomed through the trees. They crept closer . . . and closer . . . until they saw . . .

Cowslip Cow with her head
stuck in a fence!

"Oh, Posy, I'm so glad to
see you!" Cowslip cried.
"I squeezed through here to
reach some tasty clover, and
now I'm trapped. It's terrible!
Please help me!"

Posy and the ducks pulled
and pushed, and pushed and
pulled – but Cowslip was
stuck fast!

Moo

"I'll never get out!" howled
Cowslip. "My head will drop
off! Help me, Posy!"

"The farmer will rescue you!" said Posy. So they all cried out at the tops of their voices.

"HELP! HELP! HELP!" But the farmer was with Harry Horse in the stable, too far away to hear.

"I knew it!" wailed Cowslip. "I'm stuck here forever!" And a big tear fell from her eye with a plop!

Then, out of the corner of her eye, Posy spotted something that was sure to bring the farmer running . . .

Posy pressed the tractor's horn.

BEEEEEEEEEEEEEEEEEP!

Up the field raced the farmer!
And behind him came all the other
animals, clucking and squawking,
neighing and bleating, to see what
was happening.

"Oh dear me!" cried the farmer.
"Right, everyone. You all push, and
Harry and I will pull. After three.

One . . .

TWO . . .

THREE!"

"Heave!" gasped the animals.
"Squeeze!" shouted the farmer.
"Ooooh!" gulped Cowslip.
Suddenly there was a very
loud OOMPH!

Everybody cheered. Cowslip was free!

"Hoorah for Nosy Posy!" she mooed happily. "If it wasn't for her, I could have been stuck there forever!"

"It was nothing!" said Posy proudly.

"We'll never complain about your questions again!" the animals told Posy. "In fact, you can ask us anything you want!"

"OK! What's this for, Dilly?" Posy asked, looking at a large blue hosepipe lying nearby.

"And what happens when you turn this big handle?"

To Jason
~ NG

For Tim, good boy, well done!
~ TW

LITTLE TIGER PRESS LTD,
an imprint of the Little Tiger Group
1 Coda Studios, 189 Munster Road, London SW6 6AW
www.littletiger.co.uk

First published in Great Britain 2004
This edition published 2018

A CIP catalogue record for this book is available from the British Library